This edition first published in the United Kingdom in 1999 by
Brockhampton Press
20 Bloomsbury Street
London WC1B 3JH
a member of the Caxton Publishing Group

Reprinted 2001

Designed and Produced for Brockhampton Press by
Open Door Limited
Rutland, UK

Illustrator: F. Stocks May
Colour separation: GA Graphics Stamford

Title: BLACKBERRY FARM, Snow at Blackberry Farm
ISBN: 1-84186-004-2

SNOW AT BLACKBERRY FARM

Jane Pilgrim

Illustrated by F. Stocks May

BROCKHAMPTON PRESS

It began to snow at Blackberry Farm just before tea. Great, big, white flakes slowly covered everything. The animals peeped out to watch.

It was still snowing, when Ernest Owl looked out in the middle of the night. He watched for a little while and then went back to bed, saying to himself: "The snow will be very deep in the morning."

And it was very deep in the
morning – so deep that it
came over the top of Emily the
Goat's knees.

But very soon there were little
paths cleared all about the farm,
because Marcus Mouse came out
with his spade and Lucy Mouse
came out with her broom and they
both worked very hard.

When they had finished and were having a nice cup of tea, Joe Robin popped in. "I've just thought of Mr and Mrs Nibble," he said. "They won't be able to dig themselves out, because Mr Nibble broke his spade the other day, and I know the snow is very deep near their house. We must do something to help them."

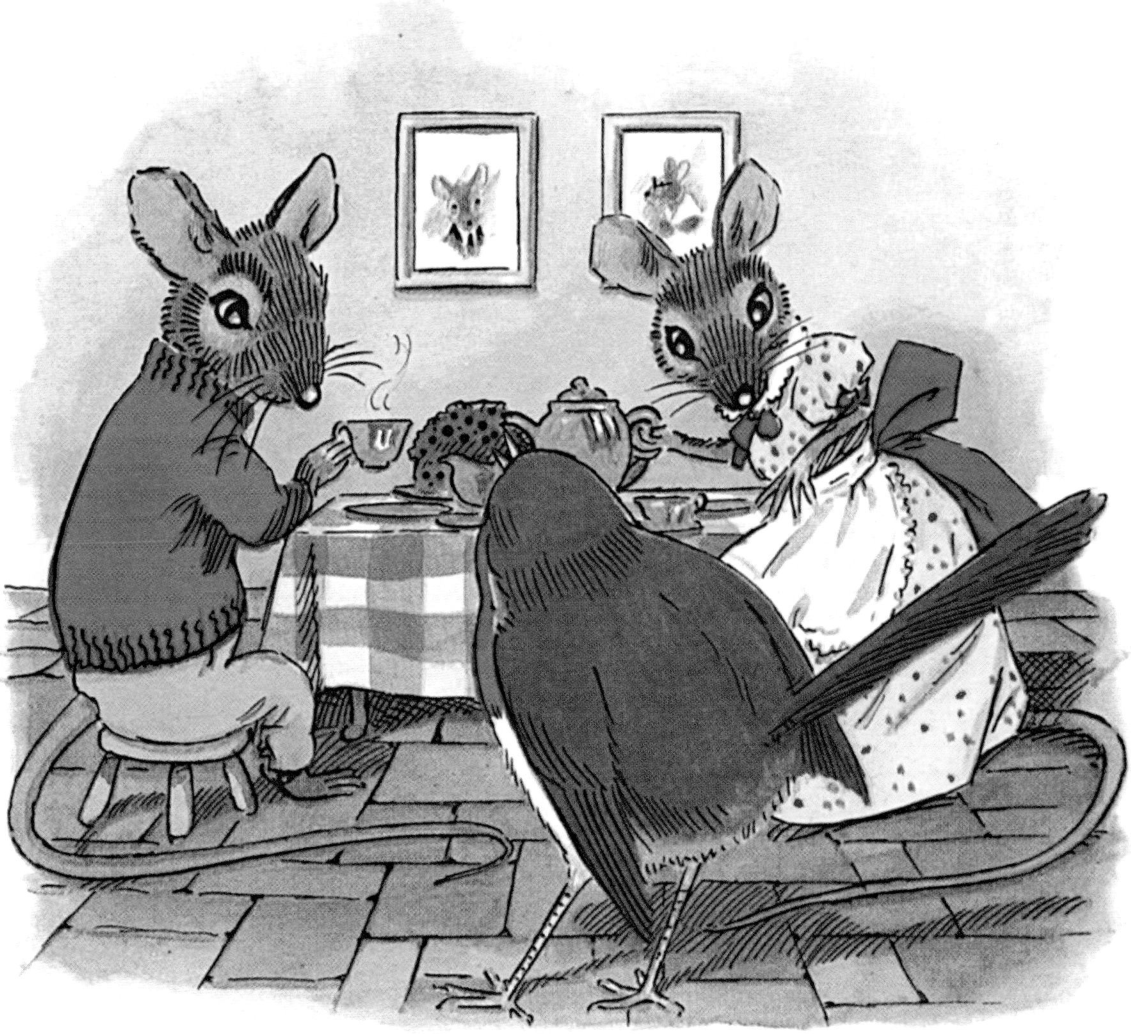

"How right you are, Joe!" cried
Lucy Moused. "We must help them
at once. You take Marcus and ask
George the Kitten to go with you.
I will pack a basket of food."
And she jumped up and hurried
them off.

Lucy Mouse fetched her basket
and put inside it a new loaf she
had just made, a pot of her best
jam and a large pat of butter.
Then she set off after the others.

George the Kitten was asleep in the stable when Joe and Marcus found him. But he woke up at once and stretched and said that he would certainly help them. "I'm very good at digging holes," he told Joe Robin, and Joe Robin said: "Thank you, George, that was why I asked you."

When Lucy Mouse reached the bank where Mr and Mrs Nibble lived with their three children, all she could see was snow. No front door, no little windows – just snow. "Oh dear," she thought. "My poor friends!" and she called very loudly: "Cheer up, cheer up! We've come to dig you out!"

Very soon Joe Robin arrived with
Marcus and George, and they all
began digging and scraping and
scratching at the snow bank,
trying to find the front door.

Ernest Owl joined them, and
suddenly his beak hit something
hard. "Quick, quick!" he hooted.
"I think I've found the window!"
and with George's help he worked
away and suddenly they saw
the window.

And peeping through the window was Mrs Nibble's smiling face. After that they found the door, and cleared some of the snow off the little step and the little path up to the door, and Mr and Mrs Nibble were able to walk out of their house.

"How very, very kind of you to
come and help us," said Mr Nibble.
"And how very, very good of you
to bring us food. We're very
hungry. Please come in and share
it with us."

So Lucy and Marcus, and Ernest
Owl and George, and Joe Robin all
went into Mrs Nibble's Kitchen,
and sat round the table and had
a big meal, because they were
very hungry too, after all their
digging. Ernest Owl said that he
could not remember when there
had ever been so much snow at
Blackberry Farm.